WHAT IF I TELL YOU?

A HEART WITH MILLION EMOTIONS

GARVIT DEVEDI

Copyright © Garvit Devedi
All Rights Reserved.

Contents

Acknowledgements

Writing a book is much difficult than I ever thought because I was always full of stories in my head but it is definitely more rewarding too than I could have ever imagined. None of this could have been possible without my family members. They were the one to always provide me with the required comfort and all the space to move on with my work. They always stood with me during every struggle and all my successes and that is I guess family is for.

I am very thankful to the people who have motivated me and pushed me to even start with the book because there were very few, friends like Vidhisha had believe on my ideas much before I even had one.

I will be eternally grateful to my little sister, Pallavi, who was always there for me. She taught me discipline, gave me honest feedback, and always pulled me up when my life was full of ups and downs.

Throughout the process of writing a book about such a story, I had a surreal experience. I will be eternally grateful to my family for their support and encouragement.

Prologue

A story does not begin with words, in my opinion; it all begins in our hearts.

Our hearts contain a million emotions, and each heart has its own story. The story has a similar heart, one that is deeply passionate and profoundly complex. It is a relationship between two people that transcended borders and imaginations.

When the stars conspired for them, the situation began to unravel; they all made mistakes and moved on, but when things are planned by the universe, they happen in the best way possible.

The story is not his, hers, or mine; rather, it is a story for all. It reflects what is going on around you, possibly with you or in your neighbourhood. It begins to disintegrate as we learn more about the characters.

I
THE JOURNEY

"Have you packed your medicines?", Shravan asked in an irritated tone.

Dhruv responded, "I forgot and they aren't required; I am perfectly fine, look !!"

Shravan is usually angry with him because of his carelessness with his own things; his job is to keep all of his appointments but is more than just a secretary to him, and he is really concerned about him like his family.

"Sometimes I wonder how you established such a big company while still not being your own self," Shravan reprimanded.

He was scolding him and all the while Dhruv is busy packing his all the other stuffs, he is starring his tickets, totally into some deep thoughts like it is all that is existing for now. A different kind of spark is in his eyes starring the tickets as if this flight will take him to heaven.

"Now what are you finding in the tickets, I am not leaving you alone this year."

Dhruv reacted like he didn't even hear him, lastly, he kept his diary and he finished his packing.

Flight is on time today they both left together for the airport, in the waiting area Shravan is all into the presentation he has with the client for a huge collaboration for their business and is sharing all the details with him but Dhruv's eyes are stuck on the clock waiting for the plane to arrive. He is absolutely somewhere else in his mind and this isn't the first time with Shravan where Dhruv is lost in his own thoughts and ignores business talks.

"Flight will come on its time; it won't take off early if you stare the clock" Shravan said to bring him back from his thoughts.

"And what is the thought that always rules your head, I have been tired of asking this. I simply don't understand what is so involving you "Shravan asked

"The emptiness, I think of the void that can't be filled in my life no matter what I do" Dhruv replied without even turning his face.

Shravan asks him that what is lacking?

You have everything, what is the thing you can't buy? you have such a huge business, a successful life and you rule the Forbes cover. Though you lost your parents at a very early age but you made everything on your own, you did what you wanted achieved what you had to. What else one can dream for?

As always all of his practical questions remain unanswered by Dhruv and it's time to go. They both sat in the plane and it took off on time. Shravan is busy with his last-minute presentation and Dhruv catches some sleep where he dreams about his childhood memories.

He was just 12, after his parents passed away, he was taken care by his grandparents who loved him a lot but couldn't do much because of their old age.

He was sent to a boarding school in Shimla where his grandfather could somehow managed to pay his fees from his small bakery. His grandparents could hardly manage to make food for themselves so had to take this tough decision.

Life was very harsh to him at this early age which made him extremely introvert and he landed up to place where everyone already had friends and groups and he used to sit quietly in the corner bench and usually sketching. He didn't like the place, he usually used to sit under a mango tree in the campus playground from where he saw all other students playing and giggling around but he went unnoticed and that killed his social confidence. He hated his grandparents to send him here, he mostly returned empty stomach from the break.

Gradually this continued for a month now for his struggle and because of his introvert behaviour, he never approached anyone in the class nor did they. He started feeling lonely and somewhat depressed too. He started blaming God because he snatched his parents from him and in return have him no friends to even talk too.

One day Miss Julie was not present for the class and they got a period off, where everyone got excited with the news and got busy into gossiping and playing around Dhruv was upset with the fact that for another hour he will have to sit alone. At least when there's some teacher teaching in the class it would keep his mind engaged.

He had nothing to do, so he took out his small sketch book and began to scribble something into it when he was suddenly hit by someone who pushed him to the bench's corner and sat next to him.

This was his first encounter with her, and it was the first time he noticed her. Somaira was a girl with short hair, brown eyes, and cherry-coloured cheeks. Actually, she was playing a game with her friends when she ran away from one of them and sat beside him. Since he started at the school, no one has ever sat next to him. He couldn't take his gaze away from her captivating smile and couldn't stop himself from staring at her, whereas she was so busy gossiping with her friends that she didn't even bother to look back to see who was sitting next to her.

After a while, the bell rang, and the teacher arrived for the next class, and everyone returned to their seats. He had no idea she sat in the seat directly in front of him in the parallel row before that.

The face of her cannot be forgotten, since then Dhruv's eyes could always find her in the class. He used to stare her smile or sometimes doing silly actions of copying teachers while they were teaching which kept him engaged throughout the day. Now for no reason he used to leave some space on his seat and sit slightly on the corner side hoping someday she would come and sit again next to him. Now his days were not so boring like earlier and classes felt much better.

He arrived a little late for his science class one day, and the teacher was already there.

"May I come in ma'am?" he asked softly in scared tone.

"Yes! Come in and bring me your assignment." She replied rudely.

Today was the deadline for submitting their science assignment, but luckily, they had completed it by staying awake the previous night, so they were not concerned. While removing his project from his bag, his eyes were searching for Somaira among the rush of students constantly crossing to submit their work; when his gaze settled on her, he noticed that she appeared worried and was fighting with her bag. She was sweating and panicking as she searched her bag for something.

He was trying to figure out what happened to her and meanwhile she stood up.

"Ma'am, I mistakenly forgot to bring my assignment today" she said in numb voice

"These all are your excuses to hide your fault, you haven't made it, I am sure. If you want marks on your grade card then better submit it right here." Teacher scolded.

"Ma'am...I have..." somaira fumbled.

"Take a seat! "I'm not going to entertain such stupid excuses," the teacher said, cutting her words in between shouts.

Gradually, everyone turned in their work, and the teacher began marking it in the checklist to ensure that no one was left out. Somaira was already prepared to hear the scores, and her eyes were almost filled with tears as she realised, she would have to face the consequences.

'Harish check! Komal check! Somaira..." the teacher kept arranging and marking students.

Somaira was nervous, and her face turned pale; she had always been a bright student, and she had never had to hear scolding's, even this time she did her work.

'Somaira check!" teacher said and moved on with other names.

She was really surprised that how could it happen, she did not submit definitely the teacher made some mistake.

Soon all the names were checked except just one who didn't submit the work.

"Dhruv! where's your work?" teacher shouted asking him.

'Ma'am, I forgot" he replied in fear.

"Get out of the class! you will be marked zero for this, go stand near the gate" teacher yield at him.

Dhruv quietly exited the classroom, somewhere inside he knew this was going to happen. He actually renamed his assignment and submitted it on Somaira's behalf because he saw her in tears.

Somaira had discovered by this point that it was not a mistake on the part of the teachers. For the first time, she noticed him but was intrigued as to why he would do such a favour for her when they didn't even know each other, and she also felt very guilty because someone else was being punished for her mistake.

She dashed out the door as soon as class was over to see him.

"Dhruv? Right?" she asked

"Ah Yes!" he replied

She extended her hand to him without saying anything...

"Friends?" she asked him with a smile.

When he saw her, his eyes twinkled. He had no idea she would ask him to be her friend. He could see her up close, and she was stunning, which kept him engrossed.

• 5 •

II
THE ONLY PLAN

"Seatbelt !"

"Seatbelt sir!" Airhostess said standing near Dhruv.

The flight was about to land on the runway when he was awakened by the voice of the airhostess telling him to fasten his seatbelts for safety. They arrived in Rome, and Shravan had to travel to Milan from there.

Shravan handed him his luggage and all the necessary documents at the airport.

"See, I know you won't let me come with you, but you must promise me that you will take care of yourself and take your medications on time, every time." Shravan was sighing but was completely focused on him.

"Yes, Yes I will, I am not a kid Shravan I can take care of myself you just do well with the clients" Dhruv consoled him.

Shravan explained that he had already made all of the airport arrangements for him.

"Just outside the airport there is a black car waiting for you, the driver will take you straight to your hotel where I have booked your room and also food will be on them so no worries" Shravan was briefing him about his arrangements.

While he was explaining Dhruv was just pretending to hear everything but he was actually just nodding his head. He was just waiting for him to finish soon so that he can leave fast.

Dhruv soon left the airport, came outside and he went absolutely as per the plan but definitely not of Shravan's. So as per the plan he saw the car outside but instead of taking that he escaped in a local taxi.

"Take me to the nearest metro station" Dhruv said to the cab driver

Dhruv had no idea where he was going until now, so he decided a metro station would be a good place to start and then decide from there. His only plan was to not have any plans at all.

Soon he reached the station and seeing the trains name flashing on the screen he couldn't decide where to go, so he took the first metro which came on the platform number 2 which was going to Castelli Romani. It was a city located in the south-eastern side and a very quiet place because it was still isolated with the main city rush.

He grabbed the corner seat because that was the only seat empty and sat quietly looking outside the window. He was lost in the view seemed like with the moving platforms he could see his life moving in a bioscope Infront of his eyes. He had no clue where was the train taking him to.

III

THE ONE WITH AN OLD MAN

At the next stop, he noticed an elderly man struggling to enter. The old man was carrying so many belongings that it appeared as if he was moving his entire home somewhere.

"Shall I take some of those?" Dhruv asked the old man offering help.

The old man handed him a few bags and looked up and smiled at him as a gesture of thanks; it was clear from his innocent smile that he was grateful to him because he didn't expect anyone to help him in this world of hustle.

Dhruv escorted him to his seat and forced him to sit, while carefully storing his belongings and standing nearby.

"You don't look familiar, are you new to the city young man?" The old man asked.

"Oh yes." Dhruv replied.

The old man asked him, "where are you going? "

"If you are a traveller and have come to roam then my friend you are in the wrong train because the city is opposite to the route." The old man added.

"No, actually I am not here to travel and I... I don't like the city so It's fine." Dhruv responded.

"Are you running from something or somewhere?" the old man inquired.

"No, no, no, not at all." Dhruv was taken aback but responded.

"Are you staying in Romani? "Because there aren't many hotels out there," the old man inquired.

Dhruv till now didn't even knew where was he going so, he nodded in a No, but said that he will figure out something once he reaches.

The final station arrived and one by one everyone was stepping out of the train. Lastly, the old man was also moving out towards the gate but Dhruv was stoned and didn't move.

"Who is going to carry these heavy bags now huh?" The old man turned at him and asked in sarcasm.

Dhruv looked at him, and the man invited him to accompany him to his home until he decided where to go next.

"No, it's fine I will manage something" Dhruv denied formally.

"I am surely old but not a cranky one, don't be afraid young man" The old man laughed insisting him to come along.

He agreed somehow to go with him and took his bags again. They left from there and after a long walk and after a king like experience in a chariot they finally reached an empty grassland, it was all green wherever one can see and the scenic beauty cannot be described but was surreal.

The old man led him to a trail in the grass, and after a few minutes, he could see smoke coming from the chimneys of small cottages, and at one of them, a dog was tied outside, barking loudly when he saw them; the dog was barking in delight to see the old man, and that was his cottage.

7It was a small cottage in between the grassland, typically made of stones and wooden planks with minimum modifications done over the years.

The dog jumped at the old man and started licking him in joy to welcome him.

"Come in, young man, this is my small world, and you can stay as long as you want." The old man greets him and invites him to his home.

"I live here alone, so you can take either of the two rooms you want, now you can freshen up and soon join me for dinner," they said as they entered the house.

As they arrived, Dhruv observed the home was full with photo frames, most of which were of the same lady; he thought it weird that there were images on the wall, side table, and even bookcases.

He chose the last available room and proceeded to clean up and store his things. Soon after, he came out for dinner, and the aroma of something incredibly excellent was wafting down the corridor, making him hungry.

He received four missed calls from Shravan up to that point, which he did not return.

The old man made some kind of soup and cheese toast sticks for him. The dining table was attached to the small messy open kitchen. The old man offered him the food and they sat together to eat.

The soup was smelling really nice or maybe he thought has didn't had anyone since morning that was the reason but anyway, he tasted and in just one sip he realised how wrong he was.

"You don't have anyone living with you?" Dhruv asked to divert himself from the taste of the soup.

"I live with my wife, see up she is all around "The old man pointed to the walls and replied.

"So where is she now? She's not here?" he asked curiously.

"I don't know but she will return home soon" The old man answered.

Dhruv was perplexed as to why he was unaware of his wife's existence and had no idea where she was.

"You want some more?" the old man asked offering him some more soup.

"No No I am done" Dhruv replied.

Dhruv realised he couldn't even finish half of the soup by the time the old guy completed his and walked into the kitchen to do other things. While the old guy worked in the kitchen, Dhruv continued the discussion till he finished the soup.

"You don't know where is she then how are you so sure she will return?" he asked.

"It's a lengthy storey, young guy, and it may tyre you." Smiling, the old guy said.

"No, tell me." "All of my ears!" He responded immediately.

The elderly guy then began telling his story, stating that it was 1975 and that he recalls it vividly. He got accepted into the Air Force Academy, and it was his first solo flight; he was scared and apprehensive that day.

He also had a trainer in the back to handle any mishaps. He acquired the controls, took off, and landed successfully despite some turbulence.

As he landed on the runway and just started his celebration with all other teammates a roaring sound from the sky grabbed their attention, it was a fighter jet and the way it was surfing it the air was an immersive experience in itself.

The plane then touched down on the runway to the right. They were all so fascinated by the flying tactics in front of them that they were all waiting for the pilot's cabin to open so they could see who was actually flying the aircraft. A flight and landing with such precision were unusual for trainees like them.

The cabin door opens, and the pilot steps out, taking the helmet off his head, and everyone, including him, is taken aback. Suzi was the first person I saw, and she was a lady flying it so flawlessly. Suzi was an accomplished pilot and batch gold medallist.

"I recall her gorgeous face, the way her hair shone in the brilliant light, and how her eyes sparkled." She walked with assurance. That sight will stay with me for the rest of my life." Her wife was described by the old guy.

He then moved ahead with the story and said that she was the guest trainer invited that day specially to give them basics about jets and make them aware of the war scenario to keep them ready in all perspectives. Adam (The old man) since them, attended all the training sessions without fail but he couldn't be ready enough. One day, Suzi called him personally after the session to ask him about what is the problem with him because he seemed quite attentive and disciplined so why such lack of confidence. That day he said all, he said he knows everything but lacks confidence whenever he gets into the cabin that fear of crash or any mishap makes him nervous and then there's a mistake always.

Suzi got the nerve at once so since then each day she called him personally after sessions to help him out with his fear. Gradually in very less time span he got to learn a lot and a lot of potential within him he realised was unnoticed.

They started opening up with each other sort of liked each other's company, where Adam loved her since the first sight but soon Suzi also found his presence good. They started meeting outside the base also and got to know about each other's life.

Suzi liked Adam's innocent child like behaviour and the fact that he hides nothing. Until the last day they both spent a good time together and now they were used to each other and dependent emotionally.

On the last day keeping in mind all the beautiful moments they spent together Adam didn't wanted to be late so he decided not to miss the opportunity of proposing her right Infront of everyone in the Airbase itself. He bent on his knees and with a beautiful flower bouquet he proposed he, he could hear his beats when there was a min silence after he expressed his feelings that way and then surprisingly Suzi said a YES! it was a moment overwhelmed with joy where everyone was celebrating their togetherness. They got engaged right there before she leaves the base and that was definitely something she didn't expect to happen this way.

After that they used to meet on planned vacations and roamed across all the cities together. They spent a very lovely time of their lives together and were planning to marry soon. They always thought to settle in a small house of their own somewhere in the countryside where they live in just themselves with a dog for company and lots of birds. They wanted to hang all their moments on the walls of their house just the way that their home tells their love story to everyone who enters in there.

They had planned everything and, in a month, they had to marry. Adam was busy with all the preparations for their wedding, he had called every single person they knew to their wedding as they wanted it to be grand one.

Suzi just had a drill mission where she had to go to a nearby island practice the bomb drop and return back to the base. It was a drill with 6 women pilots and also the trail and test of a new bomb.

Adam was so enthusiastic about their wedding that he scheduled it all by himself after seeing her off. Guests were invited, outfits were coordinated, and everything was beautifully planned.

All six planes took off on time in the clear sky that morning and arrived on time with the designated path, and their successful drop was reported on the radio transmission. All of the jets were returning to the base, but only five were tallied when they landed.

Adam conducted the entire inquiry because only Suzi did not appear from drill practise that day. Adam waited for her excitedly that day, but the wait evolved into disappointment and worry. The radio controller reported that she arrived at the destination and successfully completed the operation, but they lost contact with her shortly after on the way back.

Adam broke into tears and after days of wait their wedding was cancelled, everyone believed that she had a plane crash and she's no more alive but no one could make him believe. He was very sure that she will return one day to him, he believed that she was the best pilot in the history nothing can ever happen to her.

He quit his work, cashed in all his funds, and built the house just as they had planned. He fulfilled all of their retirement dreams, including a property in the countryside, walls adorned with photo frames, and an eternal wait for his wife.

"She was the finest pilot, and she loved me so much; nothing can happen to her till I die." In a choked voice, the old man murmured.

"Phone call!" Shravan called Dhruv to check on him because he had not taken the cab or arrived at the hotel.

Dhruv was entirely engrossed in the narrative of the elderly guy, and he sipped his soup from the bowl without even tasting it.

"It's time to sleep young man." The old man said asking him to sleep.

Dhruv retired to his room to relax for a bit, but the storey of Adam had such an impression on him that it was difficult for him to think that someone could love someone so much that they would wait a lifetime for them. Before going to bed, he wrote about Adam in his diary.

Shravan dialled his number again, and this time he answered. Shravan yelled at him for his negligence, and Dhruv calmed him down, assuring him that he is well and secure, and that he is taking all of his medications on schedule.

Shravan informed him all about business and that a meeting with the customer was arranged for tomorrow, but he was uninterested in Shravan's important business matters, so he heard everything and requested Shravan to let him sleep because he had a busy day.

The next morning, he awoke with a ray of sunlight shining directly into his eyes from the window; it was already late in the morning, and the sun had set in the sky. When he got out of the room, the old guy offered him some coffee, and the old man went back to his crops, leaving Dhruv to roam around with his tiny bag pack on his shoulders.

IV
THE ONE WITH THE MAGICIAN

On his approach to the major city, he observed a lovely lady trying to sell flowers to folks passing by. Dhruv was moved by her plight because he understood what it was like to live in poverty and how tough it was to make a livelihood out there.

"How about some flowers, sir?" These are just picked, and your lady would adore them." While passing by her modest flower shop, the flower lady stopped him.

"No thanks, I have no one to give these too." He replied politely and moved on his way.

After a long walk and all the captivating sights, he rested in a café, grabbed the corner seat with just a cup of coffee and his diary on the table to pen down his random thoughts.

He was abruptly distracted by a burst of applause. A magician was doing some of his tricks for the patrons of the café. Dhruv ignored him and continued writing in his diary.

"You don't like magic." After a while, the magician returned to his stable, having seen that he was resistant to his tricks.

"No, it's nothing like that." He replied

(The magician is a very extrovert person and very self-obsessed of his tricks.)

"Hey, I am Frank" the magician introduced himself.

"Oh yes, I am Dhruv. Nice to meet you" Dhruv replied softly shaking hands.

"Are you trying to get away from something?" Frank inquired after noticing him deep in thought and sitting quietly alone in the corner.

Dhruv showed no interest in going on with a conversation with anyone but frank was very much interested to know about new people and he found Dhruv very interesting to know.

"Okay, you don't like to share first I understand to let me start with mine." Frank said seeing no response from his end.

"I wasn't always a magician; I was a robber in New York." He used to pickpocket there and has been to jail several times. He's also spent New Year's and Christmas in jail." Frank spoke up.

Dhruv hardly looked at him, but he was intrigued by his narrative.

"I met a female, and I also want to steal anything that night." It was Christmas Eve and everyone was out partying, so I stepped into a modest city house that was adorned with 80's lights. It appeared like they had many tapes wrapped around to keep it alive, but most of them were lighted up.

I walked inside the home and searched around, but I couldn't see anything worth stealing. When he couldn't locate anything valuable in the home, he went to the fridge to acquire some food to state his hunger; he didn't eat anything the rest of the day.

Meanwhile, he heard some footfall that got clearer by the second, and the lights were switched on, and I was apprehended." He continued.

"Sit down, let me bring some food for you." The girl said

"He was taken aback, but she assured him that he was not a horrible guy; it is only hunger that drives people to do anything." She understands hunger and is aware of the pain he was experiencing. She said that she works in a tiny grocery shop to make a livelihood, which is why he arrived at the wrong time to steal something because she had nothing valuable around, but she provided him what she had, which was food. He was very embarrassed of his actions and of himself. As a result, he apologised for his behaviour.

She asked me if I want her forgiveness and really am ashamed for all that I do then I should leave all the bad practices I do.

Since then, she got me along with her in the grocery shop so that I earn to live with hard work and she helped me throughout to make me a better person. She was his wife now and now they have a little cute daughter and also, it's been 7 years of being together. Seeing his talent, she encouraged him to try his hands in magic tricks and it worked, he became a magician who travels all across the globe for his events and is living a really happy life with her." Frank said.

"Wow!" said one." That's an incredible journey for you, "Dhruv responded to my question.

"So, what is the pain I sense it in you? It's your turn so tell me?? Frank enquired.

"What if I tell you?" Dhruv said, a sympathy grin on his face.

"It was great meeting you, catch you." Dhruv left the café and returned to the cabin.

V
THE EIFFEL TOWER

It was evening time and he was walking through beautiful lanes of Rome in multicoloured sky and last sight of the sun for the day.

While walking through a small market he saw a miniature Eiffel in the display of a gift shop. He stood near e display and through the clear glass display of the shop he could see through a glimpse of his first meet after school with her. That small Eiffel tower reminded of her.

It was Christmas eve and almost two years passed without a single meet with somaira, though they were good friends in school but lately lost communication.

Back in Shimla, he approached a seller at a mall about the price of a comparable Eiffel Tower, and the salesman said, "Sorry Sir! That was recently sold."

"Who purchased it?" Dhruv asked a question.

And the salesman pointed to a girl at the pay desk, which was Somaira!

"Hey Dhruv, it's been long time." Somaira waved towards Dhruv.

He couldn't believe they'd finally met after two years. He was unsure how to react since she must have forgotten all they had done in school because she was always surrounded by people and a slew of friends.

They both sat for coffee in the mall's food court, and she began telling all of her thrilling stories, all of her excellent experiences up to that point. Dhruv remained a little silent throughout the chat, simply staring at her as if he saw something out of this world, which she noticed and made him feel more at ease to communicate.

They had several wonderful conversations that day, and he learned that she recalls everything, every single incident from school, which surprised him.

Before leaving, she gave him the miniature tower, saying that it will always remind him of the soothing time we spent together and will keep our memories of friendship fresh, her gesture was similar to this before, though she had many friends throughout her life, none of them could give her the comfort to open up with everything she felt with him in just one meeting.

"Do you require anything, Sir?" The shop owner came out to question Dhruv after noticing him staring at the exhibit for quite some time.

"No no, was just walking through saw this and stopped." Dhruv denied and moved on.

When he returned home, the old man greeted him and asked him to freshen up quickly because dinner was ready. He brought some dog food for his dog, which he offered to the dog, and the dog liked it so much that he flickered his little tail and jumped on Dhruv. They got along well, and the dog became his champion after that because he also liked dogs a lot.

Soo, they sat for dinner and the old man asked him about his day, how did it go? The old man asked about the bridges, monuments and the small markets in the city. The old man also shard a lot places which are must visit around. Dhruv shared about his day, he also mentioned about the lady selling flower.

He got a call from Shravan, asked about his health and day. Dhruv consoled him saying that he is perfectly fine. Shravan was sounding a bit worried which was quite sensed by Dhruv so he enquired.

"They rejected our proposal" Shravan answered.

"I'm not sure why, but they simply turned down our proposal. I don't understand how working with us is a chance for them, and how we're offering a higher rate than the current market for an advertising firm." He expressed his displeasure.

"What was the problem, they must have said something right?" Dhruv asked

"Yes, they did. They said Something is missing "

Shravan Said.

'But What?" Dhruv Asked.

"I don't know, I simply don't" Shravan responded

Dhruv asked him to stay for another day and try to communicate what is missing, negotiate, and make a deal because, while we are an opportunity for them, their advising company is the best in the category, so close the deal with them whatever it takes.

Puts down the phone and goes to sleep.

VI

ONE WITH THE FLOWER LADY

The next morning dog was licking his hand when he woke up.

"Ahh! Young man you make up early today shall? Make something for you "the old man asked seeing him coming down stairs

"No thanks! I have to reach somewhere" Dhruv didn't want to trouble him unnecessarily.

He grabbed his backpack and went out to eat. Just like yesterday, he saw the flower lady trying to sell her flowers to everyone who passed by as he crossed the small wooden bridge over a water stream. Perhaps it was the first shop you came across as you crossed the only connecting bridge from the countryside to the main city.

"Good morning, take this flower you will have a good day I wish." The flower lady said while he was crossing her shop.

Dhruv saw her struggling just like yesterday, and he didn't like seeing people struggle so much for survival.

"Do you have lilies?" Dhruv asked this to the lady.

"OH, yes yes ... I ... have them definitely." She said in excitement because she didn't expect him to buy one.

She had sold none for the day till now.

"So, make the best bouquet you can out of them." he ordered.

The flower lady became extremely happy, and a graceful hand began picking up the best flowers to make the bouquet with all her love, which was very clearly visible through her gleaming eyes and soft smile throughout she was making it.

Generally, she does not get such customers, and most of the time she struggles to even sell some of them in order to cover her expenses.

"Yes, it's done." she said showing him a big beautiful bouquet of lilies.

He paid for the flowers, accepted the bouquet, and presented it to the lady, wishing her a pleasant day.

"Has anyone ever told you how beautiful you are? Take this from me, a beautiful bouquet for a beautiful lady." Dhruv presented it to the lady.

"For me?" she asked surprisingly.

Her eyes filled with tears because this was a once-in-a-lifetime opportunity for her. She was overcome with joy by his gesture and thanked him profusely.

"It's okay, ma'am; you're doing a fantastic job spreading love throughout the city." Dhruv told her to stop crying.

She asked him where he came from because he had never seen him before.

"Actually, I came from India just to explore the city, and now I'm going to look for some good breakfast," Dhruv replied.

"Breakfast? You haven't done it yet?" she asked.

"No, I was actually lost near the lane, but I'm going to grab something now." He responded.

"Hey, I'm Laura and just behind I have my place." She said introducing herself and pointing towards her home.

The lady then insisted with him to join her for breakfast at her home, which was right behind the flower shop; she was going to have breakfast, so she said she would be delighted to have him as her guest.

Dhruv denied, but she wouldn't let him go, so he had no choice but to agree. They went to her small cosy place, which had only one room and pictures of her daughter on the walls. The house was not well furnished, but everything was in its place and nicely done.

She offered him a seat near the attached kitchen and some food.

They began with breakfast and casually discussing her family, and he inquired as to where her daughter was.

She mentioned that her family owned a small business and that they were well-off, but that they no longer like her.

"Why? Whom do you live here with?" Dhruv asked.

She stated that she lives in this rented house with her daughter and gets her bread and butter from the small flower shop in the front. She became teary-eyed when she spoke about her husband.

Dhruv asked "what happened to him?"

"He left" she murmured.

"But why? I don't see any flaw in you then what happened?" Dhruv was shocked to know.

She told him that she ran with the guy leaving her family against their will a married him but soon all the love vanished from their relationship. One year later she got pregnant and she shared her happiness wit her husband as she felt this could be the reason to settle everything between them, this news would heal all their scars but unfortunately it didn't happen her way. Her husband reacted absolutely shocked and he wasn't ready to take responsibility of a child and became a father at such an early age so they had a massive argument over this but she was rigid on the point, she wanted to bring her baby in the world.

And it was for this reason that he abandoned her at a time when she needed him the most. He ran away from all of his responsibilities, and because I married against my family's wishes, they are angry with her, and she is not even welcome in her own home.

She managed to rent this place with all of her savings and get a room to stay behind the shop so that he can also take care of her daughter with the shop. She had been juggling her expenses, her daughter's education, and her erratic income since then. She mentions that because of the fierce competition in the market, she is struggling to keep up with her fees and the house rent.

"don't know how long will I be able to keep things tied." She shared.

"But anyway, that's my part, I saw a diary in your hand. Are you a writer?" she asked smiling.

"What me? No, I just scribble my thoughts on it" he said.

"Then definitely I would love to hear some of them if you agree." She insisted him to recite something from his diary.

After denying a couple of time he opened his diary and started turning pages for a few seconds.

"Okay, this will be fine I guess" he said stopping on one page.

"Weaving a rope!

Weaving a poem for you,

Weaving a rope to bind us together,

Weaving with the thread of love and needle,

Comforting your soul beneath and woollen riddle.

There's a compass directing,

To my person in the middle.

Interlacing the textures,

To craft the hues, I fiddle.

Holding you close,

Was a fountain on your baby skin.

I smile and cradle,

On your nightmare and the lovely spin.

You are the one,

to rip my frustrations from within.

You are my few drops,

On the grass of my skin.

I'm writing the words,
To web and pour my thoughts.
Like the wools are woven,
With its beautiful knots.
Today, I wrote a poem for you,
Knitting each word carefully,
So that it may whisper in your ears gracefully." He recited.

Her little daughter, who was standing near the door, began clapping; she had arrived from her classes while he was reciting and had enjoyed his poem. Laura was engrossed in the poem, and she adored him.

"Wow, it was really beautiful but I find this one is definitely for someone, maybe someone special." Laura appreciated.

"I...I actually imagined anything and wrote, I told you that I scribble anything." Saying this Dhruv got up to keep the dishes and to avoid further questions.

Meanwhile, in a rush, he shook the table, causing a diary to fall to the floor. Laura picked up the diary, kept it on the table, and noticed a picture fall from it on the floor.

Dhruv instantly picked it up and kept it back in his diary.

"I guess I've seen her somewhere," Laura murmured, trying to recall something.

"What her? No way." He replied.

"NO, I haven't," she said confidently this time.

Dhruv was perplexed, so he took out the picture again and handed it to her, asking her to recall it correctly.

"Oh Yes! She lives right here behind the grassland." She said shouting in confidence as she cracked some kind of code.

"Really?" Dhruv asked multiple timers reassuring that it was her and this time his eyes was filled.

It was Somaria's picture, and he hadn't seen her in 6 years, and now he was right next to her.

"Yes, but she looked a little different now, which is why it took me so long to remember." Her hair is now shorter than it was in the photo. "She used to take one flower and place it above her ears every day, I remember," she said of her.

"Can you tell me where is she?" Dhruv asked impatiently.

"I haven't seen her since few days but she told me she lives somewhere in the colony just behind the grass fields" she added.

Dhruv immediately ran leaving everything over there.

"But...but how do you know her?" Laura shouted from behind but until then he ran away.

He ran across the bridge and through the grasslands, holding her photograph in his hand. Soon after, at the end of the fields, he noticed some chimneys and houses, and he ran madly, showing her picture to everyone he could see and inquiring about her.

But after hours of search, he still couldn't find any clue to get to her. Meanwhile Shravan was calling him but everything was unheard in that moment. He was only concerned about finding any trace of her if she is there.

He did all he could asked people, looked himself and everything. He got tired and he was sweating heavily, soon in the middle of grasslands he felt dizzy and fainted. There was no one near who could see him and help, he came far from the market and in the search of her he came in the middle of the field where his unconscious body was hidden in long blade like golden grasses.

VII
THE DIARY TELLS YOU ALL

Laura was keeping all his stuffs safely as he left all of them at her home itself. She was very curious to know what is the connection and how does he know that girl. She couldn't resist herself from reading his diary.

On ethe very first page of her diary she found a dried lily below that was written "from nature to a beauty of nature" dated 16th July 2011.

This tickled her to read more about him and she kept turning pages, the very next page was 29th July 2011.

" Today was my first day at the collage and went pretty well, I learned a lot of things, met a lot of people and most importantly I felt like a grownup today. It felt a whole new start to an all-new phase of my life.

I wasn't happy uselessly, it around a year now since we reunited after schooling and fortunately, we were in the same collage. I got to know she is going to soon join the collage and that gives me butterflies in my head. 10-year-old me is so amused to know that we will be around in the came campus all over again just like the school days mostly all the time from now."

Laura continued to read his diary, and she gradually learned more about him. Dhruv and Somaira began spending a lot of time together by this point and were enjoying each other's company. They realised how comfortable they were with each other, and Somaira began to like him. The feeling was nothing new for Dhruv, but this time it came from her, and the warmth of emotions was equal on both ends.

One day, almost after a year she confessed her love for Dhruv and from a minute he got nothing to say, absolutely speechless because no where in his dreams he imagined something like this to happen.

He mentioned it was the 4th of May that year, and they had an argument about something he can't even remember, and she accidentally ended up confessing her feelings for him. In his heart, an unforgettable memory was formed that no one knew would live on for the rest of his life.

Dhruv and somaira both were very passionate about their career. They wanted to be something and they also had the spark to do so. It won't be wrong to say that the passion, determination and the dedication towards his dreams was something somaira really admired in him and loved the most about him.

They both dreamed together, big but cosy dreams. They began to live in the imaginary dream they had created for themselves, which was so real that they didn't care about people or the world around them.

Dhruv and Somaira were inseparable by that point; they used to travel, eat, and live carefreely with each other, and they gradually forgot everything. He was no longer lonely; instead, no one would believe he was the same silent boy from school, but he used to laugh, speak a lot, and enjoy all the little things he used to do.

Laura got so indulged into their story that She read all the poems he wrote for her and felt like emotions were flowing through the pages.

She turned the pages and continued reading slowly, page by page, until she came to a blank page, and to continue reading, she flipped all the pages after that, but they were all white, and all the pages after that were blank.

When Dhruv opened his eyes, he noticed the dog licking his hands. He was brought to the old man's house and was lying on the couch in the hallway.

Actually, while the old man was out walking his dog, the dog smelled Dhruv and tracked him down among the long grasses, where he was brought back to his home.

"Are you fine young man?" the old man asked.

"Yes, just feeling a little dizzy." Dhruv responded.

Old man offered him something to drink, "Drink this! you'll feel much better."

He also informed Dhruv that he was receiving calls from someone named Shravan on a regular basis, so he picked up the phone and informed him of his condition. Shravan was on his way to Rome to see him after hearing that he had fainted, and he could arrive anytime soon, as he informed.

Dhruv didn't want Shravan to come, so he called him back to stop him, but in the meantime, he arrived at the location to look for him.

"I told you not to go alone but you never hear me out, now see what happened." Shravan fired up at him as so he entered.

Dhruv reassured him that he was on his way back to Shimla without further delay.

Dhruv tried to persuade him that he had to find Somaira no matter what it took, but as soon as he took his, medicines, and a bowl of soup, he put on his jacket and was ready to go out and look for her again.

"Now would you tell me where are you going" Shravan shouted on him to stop him.

"Please let me go, Shravan; I have to go." Dhruv requested that he let him go.

"Do you even care about your health and what is so necessary?" Shravan asked in pissed off mood.

"What if I tell you?" Dhruv said looking straight into Shravan's eyes.

His eyes ere so deep and filled with some strange spark which Shravan never noticed ever before.

"I am looking for my life and it is more important to me than my own life." Dhruv said and left.

Dhruv left the place this time his eyes couldn't be ignored Shravan couldn't even utter something so he followed Dhruv on his way at least to ensure his safety.

Dhruv went straight to Laura to find any more clue to get to her, any trace that could lead him closer to Somaira because he couldn't find any himself.

"Laura do you...do you know anything else, any sign that could take me to her..." Dhruv asked to Laura while he was breathing heavily as he ran from there to her.

"Wish I could help but I really don't know anything" Laura said in disappointed tone.

Laura then returned all of his belongings, including his diary. Dhruv was dissatisfied and sat down on the street side. Laura entered the room and sat quietly beside him. She also apologised for reading his diary without his permission and asked him politely, "What happened on November 3rd, and why is his diary blank from there?"

Dhruv was overcome with emotion at the time, and he simply whispered that he had lost everything all at once.

"Why? What happened and what happened to her?" Laura asked him.

Laura then returned all of his belongings, including his diary. Dhruv was dissatisfied and sat down on the street side. Laura entered the room and sat quietly beside him. She also apologised for reading his diary without his permission and asked him politely, "What happened on November 3rd, and why is his diary blank from there?"

Dhruv was overcome with emotion at the time, and he simply whispered that he had lost everything all at once. On that day, he claimed to have learned that Somaira's family had forced her to marry someone of their choosing, which she had been ignoring for quite some time. They were also aware of our relationship, so they did not agree with us on this. Soon after, she became engaged to someone else, and the news completely rocked him to his core. He tried every possible method of communication with her, but it was futile.

They both were unhappy with the decision but they always wanted to move on further only with their parents' consent. After a week he got to know she was secretly engaged in a small temple with only few close and important relatives and after a year he had to marry. Through a common friend of there he got a few pictures of the ceremony and that shook him and all the dreams they lived together were shattered even without coming into existence.

Somaira called him that evening, and he answered right away. That entire evening, they cried over call until their eyes dried up. That day, two beautiful hearts were murdered, and once again, a pure emotion was unable to reach its destination.

It was a heart-breaking end to another beautiful journey. They never expected it to end this way; they could recall all the promises they made for the rest of their lives, all the moments and all the small little habits they had with each other.

That was the last time he could hear her and she asked him not to stop from here and move on for his own self, for good. She wanted to see him to really good place.

"It ended as it had to be and we will have to live with it, its not always our choice Dhruv...!" these were her last words.

"But then why are you here? How did you know you will find her here?" Laura asked him.

"Because she always used to say whenever she is lost and I can't find her I should come to Rome and knock at the cottages. She said you will find me here in a small cottage of wood which is just surfeit for two and she will always wait for him to search for her." Dhruv explained her that though he knows now they can't be together but he promised he will definitely come here, so he came here to feel her close.

"Wow!"

"I'm not sure if I should call you crazy or out of this world, but one thing is certain: I haven't seen such pristine love and emotions in a long time, and it's difficult to believe such pure love still exists." Laura was taken aback.

Laura was astounded by his love passion and devotion to a single person, even though he knows they are poles apart and can never be reunited.

Shravan asks Dhruv to fly back to India because he now knows all the reasons for Dhruv's behaviour and all the questions, he had for him for years have been answered all at once.

Shravan insisted on his return because there is nothing left to do here now, the deal they came for has been cancelled, and he couldn't find her despite his best efforts, so staying here for too long will be emotionally and physically exhausting for Dhruv. He also advised Dhruv to move on from this and resume his life, focusing on himself and his health, because even if he found a way to her, it would be completely futile because she is married. It's better to live peacefully and not disrupt her life by bringing her past into the present.

Dhruv somehow got convinced by his thought, he collected himself up and was ready to fly back. His action was over now he again wanted to keep himself engaged all day with the outer world to keep himself distracted from his inner self because that what he knows and is practicing for so long.

VIII
THE MEET

He decided to pick up where he left off, so he first asked Shravan to contact the company with which they had to deal. Shravan simply refused because he knew Dhruv was not in a mental state to work, and they are not professional in rejecting proposals without a valid reason.

"Shravan, are you connecting the call?" Dhruv ordered him to do so.

The call connected with the company's CEO.

"Hello! "Dhruv said.

"I was expecting your call, but a bit early." CEO responded.

Dhruv asked straight away what was the problem with the proposal and what was lacking in the presentation or quotation, if any, we can negotiate on that part.

"Nothing was wrong with the proposal" The CEO responded.

"Then? what was the issue?" Dhruv questioned.

"It's your bouquet." The CEO reacted.

"What? Bouquet? what can be wrong in a bouquet and how is it effecting the deal?" Dhruv asked surprisingly.

"Your bouquet lacked lilies; Dhruv, you know I only like lilies." She (CEO) responded politely.

Dhruv was numb for a while as if he is trying to believe something but couldn't. he can believe what he was feeling and his hands went cold and face red.

"Soma...Somaira? Is that you" he asked in chocked voice.

"Huhh! Finally, what took you so long?" Somaira asked.

Dhruv's eyes welled up with tears and his throat tightened; he couldn't believe what had just happened to him. Somaira was the owner and CEO of the advertising firm with whom they had agreed to work. Laura was correct about her; she used to live there for a while before moving to Milan.

"You wouldn't like to meet?" she asked him.

"Yes, yes I am coming right away to you to Milan." Dhruv responded in excitement.

"No, not here." Somaira said.

"Then?" he asked.

"I'll be waiting for you at 5 p.m. the next day on the exact spot where it all began." She spoke up.

Dhruv knew where he needed to go, but he didn't want to miss out on this opportunity, so he wrapped everything and asked Shravan to make all the arrangements because they needed to leave soon in order to arrive on time.

Dhruv was always smiling, and he could see the charm and happiness on this face. Shravan was overjoyed but worried at the same time because she was now married and things were very different; he was worried that Dhruv would hurt himself again.

Dhruv was overjoyed like he'd never been before, and Shravan rejoiced in his joy because he hadn't seen him smile in years.

While they were about to leave Laura stopped them and handed him a flower saying "This will be my best wishes for you and I hope this time everything will end well."

From there, they took the first flight to Shimla. Dhruv took his car and drove straight to a small park in the old city; it was 5 p.m. by then, and he ran inside the park until he came to a halt; he was breathing heavily, but his eyes were searching all around for one face, the face of his dreams. His gaze was drawn to the pedestal in the far corner.

She was sitting right on the pedestal they used to sit and have talked a million times, shared thought emotions and dreamt a hundred dreams together.

His feet were frozen, and his eyes were filled with tears. He was seeing her just a few feet away after 6 long years of waiting, and now that she is here, his feet aren't moving; it felt like the world had stopped and time had frozen. He doesn't want to lose sight of a million emotions as well as the reward for his selfless devotion.

He moved in closer and sat beside her; she didn't even look up, and he was staring at her as if by magic. That was exactly like a child gazing at the stars in the sky. The moment had a lot to say, but no one could say it; there were a hundred questions to be asked, but no one cared.

"How are you?" breaking the silence, Somaira asked him.

Both of their eyes were filled with tears, and despite the fact that he had nothing to say, his eyes were reflecting everything like a mirror.

"I...I never imagined I'd be able to see you again." Dhruv murmured.

They began the conversation by talking about what they didn't want to talk about. No one could tell from a distance that they hadn't even spoken to each other in a long time.

They talked about their careers, families, and relived many memories with their friends, they cried together, and they laughed together remembering all the silly things they did in the past.

"Its time to go Dhruv!" somaira stood up and said with a smile.

Dhruv didn't want to let go of this moment; he didn't want time to pass or her presence to fade away.

"You...

"You didn't tell me about your husband; how is he doing?"

Somaira looked at him carefully and after a long silence responded "What if I tell you that I never got married."

Dhruv didn't know he heard it right or was just his imagination, "How? I mean your marriage was fixed and you already got engaged I saw pictures."

Somaira then revealed that while it was true that she was forced to marry someone by her parents, she could never accept anyone as her partner and fled her home after only a few days.

She couldn't convince her parents so lastly, she had to run from all of them and that day she directly came to his place but she saw that his house was locked. When she enquired about Dhruv in the neighbourhood, she just got to know that you left the place forever and nobody knows where. She tried calling him like a hundred times but even after days his phone of switched off.

She was completely disappointed; she ran from her house without even thinking anything just with a hope to start everting from then beginning with Dhruv but now she lost him and her hope together.

Her savings were about to run out, so she needed to start working in an advertising agency right away. Almost a year later, she received a call from Dhruv, and she returned to see him, but she also learned that he had started a new venture, a business of his own, which was flourishing and he had immediate success.

Somaira stated that she has always admired him for his great passion and dedication to achieving his lofty goals. But she realised that during their time together, he almost lost all of these; he gradually became distracted from all of his dreams, and instead, his life began to revolve around her all of the time, and all of his decisions were based on her. She also complained to him about it, and they had many arguments about it, but it was inextricably linked to him, and his entire focus was on her.

"I can't tell you how I came to a halt as I walked closer to you, or how difficult and painful that decision was for me." She was overcome with emotion.

Then she made a huge decision because she felt it was better for Dhruv if she stayed away from him, and she felt that with time, he would get over her and become more involved in his career and growth. She never wanted to be a hindrance to his success.

Later, her company offered her a position in Italy, where she went and learned a lot in her field in a very short time, and she always wanted to come to Italy, as he knows. She was able to persuade some investors after a few months of experience, and she then established her own firm. She stated that she worked 14 hours a day to achieve this and that she is now one of the best in her field.

After so many years, I received a proposal for collaboration from your company as well. She had expected Dhruv to attend the meeting when it was scheduled. She, too, had no idea they would meet in this manner, but the world is a small place. The fact that he still loves her so much, perhaps even more than before, surprised her.

"But why haven't you approached me all these years?" Dhruv asked, regretfully.

"I told you that I thought you had a life to lead now and goals to achieve, and you were growing like never before when we were together, so I didn't want to be a shackle on your legs," Somaira explained.

Dhruv had no idea she was right; he actually forgot everything when he had her, not because he lost his ambitions, but perhaps because he felt he already had everything and nothing was lacking in him.

Somaira looked up at his face to explain herself further, but saw that he was bleeding profusely.

"Hey, why is your nose bleeding?" she got worried.

"Oh! It's nothing" he said assuring her and wiped his nose.

She became very concerned about him when he fainted on the ground. She requested assistance, summoned an ambulance, and drove him to the hospital. She wasn't expecting this, and seeing doctors and nurses scurrying around him heightened her anxiety. She had no idea what had occurred.

Seeing the situation, she panicked and called Shravan informing him about all the situation and he came running to the hospital leaving everything aside.

"What happened to him and how? Shravan reached and asked her.

"I don't know we were just talking a suddenly he fainted after his nose started bleeding." Somaira informed him

"Doctor! he is fine right? Everything is alright?... Say something?" Shravan fired up on doctor as soon he came out of the examination room.

"Situation is under control but..." Doctor replied.

"But? But what doctor tell me" Shravan asked in fear.

"The situation is under control for the time being, but the time has come, and I hope your area is aware of his medical history." Doctor said this while placing his hand on Shravan's shoulder to comfort him.

"Time? What time was he referring to? He's fine, isn't he?" Shaking Shravan, Somaira inquired.

Shravan whispered," everything is over"

Shravan then revealed to Somaira that Dhruv has CAD (coronary artery disease). He has been suffering from this disease for 6 years. He had his first attack in November of that year, and after multiple diagnoses, he discovered that his arteries had narrowed, limiting blood flow to his heart.

We went everywhere, all over the world, but this disease is incurable, and we are doing everything we can to keep him alive as long as possible.

"He was never good at taking his medications on time." I had to chase him all the time." Shravan burst out crying.

Somaria's heart broke as she realised what had happened.

They were both looking for Dhruv, and while Shravan was handling all of the hospital's formalities, Somaira was constantly praying to the creator for a miracle.

It had been 12 hours, but Dhruv was still unconscious, and Somaira was curious about everything that had happened after her. She inquiries about Shravan's past.

"I don't know much because he never shares anything with a anyone but one thing was sure that time was always harsh on him."

He stated that the year he was diagnosed with this disease, the following year he lost his grandparents, one by one, first his grandfather and then his grandmother, and he was all alone in this world. He left everything and moved from Shimla to Nainital, where his grandparents lived for about a year, isolating himself from the rest of the world, he only faced losses and that was the worst phase of his life, that time triggered his disease more because there was no one to look after him.

He then recovered and stood up; believe me, he is a brave man. His grandfather owned a small bakery in the market, which was his ancestor's business, and he carried on the family tradition. I used to work with his grandfather in his bakery, and when he reopened it, I was the first to return, which is how I met him. I had no idea he had become so important to me recently. He means a lot to me, and why not? He trusted me so much as a regular employee at his small bakery that he brought me all the way to here, where I now manage a business worth billions of dollars. He never let go of my hand and pulled me up so much, and now look where he is.

Everything was now up and running. Samaria's eyes were like a film in a bioscope. She understood what had happened, why his house was locked when she returned, and why she couldn't reach him. He never forgot her, and he always answered all of her questions.

Somaira felt very guilty; she felt she was responsible for everything that had happened in his life, and most importantly, she wasn't even there with him when he was going through so much.

She had always believed that her love was above all else, but a guy here was redefining love.

And finally, after 18 hours and 36 minutes Dhruv opened his eyes and said his first words, "So...Somaira"

"Who is Somaira here?" the nurse asked peeing out of the ICU.

"Me!" somaira responded quickly.

The nurse informed her that the patient has regained consciousness and is looking for her so she can visit him inside.

Meanwhile, Doctor went outside to look for Shravan. He appeared to be a bit series, so Shravan panicked and began questioning him.

He is fine now, according to the doctor, but only for the time being. Unfortunately, there is no cure for this disease. He can live for up to 6 months with proper treatment and care, but no longer.

"You can take him home but he needs complete bedrest and a lot of attention 24x7." Doctor said.

Shravan knew this had to happen one day, but he kept his fingers crossed that a miracle would happen and he would recover unexpectedly.

IX

A FAIRY TALE STORY

Dhruv got a discharge and Shravan told everything to Somaira and both were breaking within but pretended like everything was fine Infront of him

"Okay, if this is fate, we'll face it, and this time I'm with him; he's been through a lot, but not anymore." Shravan was overcome with emotion as Somaira spoke to him.

Samaria's words were very promising; she said that no matter how many days he has, she will always be there for him; it was her loss that she couldn't spend much time with someone who only loved her.

They returned, and Somaira began living with Dhruv. They lived in Shimla in a small house that was only big enough for two people. They did everything they could think of, from climbing mountains to sitting on a cliff, decorating their house by themselves, gardening together, and dancing whenever they wanted in the house.

(It is true that everything you wish for will come true someday.)

They lived their days as if they were in their own fairy tale. Dhruv was overjoyed with her, and once she realised how much he adored her, she felt blessed every day to have someone like him. His loneliness came to an end with her; his long wait was not in vain.

They had a thousand lily plants in their garden just outside their house, and Dhruv used to love taking care of them. Somaira and he used to spend most of their evenings there, under the sky, in the cold breeze, with the smell of lilies soothing their minds.

They also proved the doctors who predicted his death wrong. Dhruv lived for three years and was completely healthy, requiring only a few medications. He did everything he wanted without any limitations, he participated in all sports, and he celebrated life with Somaira every day. They created a thousand new memories for a lifetime.

Dhruv left all of his business to Shravan and lived a better life than he could have imagined. Somaira used to tease him for confidently singing songs with incorrect lyrics, and he used to love it when she corrected him, or you could say he did it on purpose.

Shravan had never seen him so happy; whenever he came to visit, he heard Dhruv laughing and always chirpy, which occasionally brought tears to Shravan's eyes. He had wished for Dhruv's happiness for years, but now that he has it, his life is uncertain.

Dhruv used to sit outside on a rocking chair with usually a cup of coffee and his diary, he used to write about life and happiness. His habit of writing diary each day was again into practice.

X

THE LEGACY OF JOY

Shravan came to visit Somaira after Dhruv died, living all his life, maybe a little less day by day, but with millions of joyful memories. She was packing her belongings and preparing to return to Milan. He was glad she got to spend a few years with Dhruv, a man who lived solely to love her. Living in the same house with all of her memories will be difficult for her now, so she decides to return, but Dhruv will always be alive in her heart.

Her life had completely changed now that she had so many happy memories to recall, including his laughs and all the songs he dedicated to her. She discovered the proper way to love someone.

"Do you still think you can go? Because I doubt." Shravan handed her some papers and spoke.

"What is it?" she asked

Shravan asked her to come along with him as he wanted to show her something before, she makes up her mind to leave. He drove her to a place not quite far from the city abound 1 hour drive, a place which seemed like a school at first sight.

She asked, "why here?"

Shravan just asked her to have patience, "in a while you will know everything" he said.

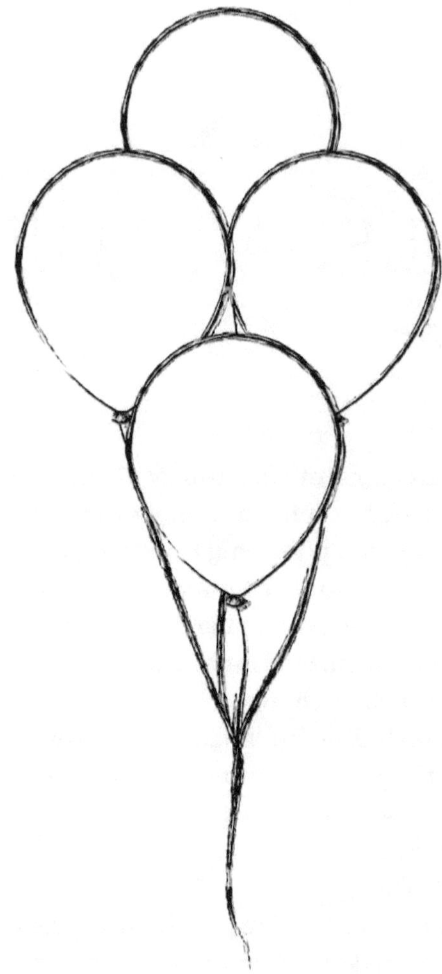

They both got out of the car and went to the front door. Shravan handed her a bouquet of balloons and a box of chocolates, saying she'd need them soon.

"Now read the papers I handed you" Shravan asked her to open the file and read.

She was perplexed as to what was going on; he took her to a school, handed her papers, and then these chocolates and balloons.

While she was reading the papers, Shravan informed her that this is a non-profit organisation that cares for orphan children, providing them with food, shelter, and education. It was founded by Dhruv, who has been doing this for a long time, and approximately 40% of his company's profits are invested in it; currently, there are 300 children staying here who are now your responsibility.

Somaira looked up at him in disbelief, having read the papers that stated that this orphanage had always been in her name and that Dhruv was just taking care of it as a manager over there. After his death, she was responsible for all of the sharers, bonds, property, and the orphanage.

It was difficult to keep her emotions in check because even when he wasn't physically present in this world, he continued to teach her the lessons of love.

A little girl ran straight to Shravan; he used to come there all the time with Dhruv, so children are familiar with him, and seeing chocolates and balloons in Somaira's hands, she couldn't help but ask, "Are these for me?"

For a split second, Somaira's eyes were filled with expectation, seeing that 5yearold little smile holding her dress and waiting for a response, her eyes expected something, they had a hope in them that couldn't be ignored.

Somaira sat down and hugged that little girl, "not only for you I have a lot for all your friends" she gave chocolates and a balloon to her.

That was a sign that she was staying and agreeing. Somaira took care of all those children just like Dhruv used to, and the business was still run by Shravan with little interference.

Somaira moved to Shimla, and her fear of loneliness vanished because she now had 300+ family members to care for. Dhruv could always be felt in the breeze, his scent lingered in their garden, and he lived in those hundred innocent smiles with her.

Laura was just following her daily routine and setting up her shop for the morning one day about a month later. She checked her mailbox for regular mail, and that day she received a letter from India, which surprised her.

When she opened the letter, it stated that the shop she used to run, as well as the house she rented, had been given to her in her name. Dhruv gave her this as a gift because he was moved by her struggle for a living and felt that this small gesture could help her.

Laura cried that day, knowing that such a man was no longer in this world, and she distributed all of the flowers for free that day in his homage.

She was overcome with emotion to see someone who cared so much for a stranger when her family never checked on her; such a soul is no longer with them. Her daughter's education was fully funded by his company, and she was permanently relieved of the financial burden of rents and struggle for expenses.

A single heart can hold a million emotions, and each heart has its own story to tell, so instead of spreading hatred, tell stories of love and humanity.

Epilogue

Many seasons passed after he died, but he lived on in the smiles of hundreds.

Somaira lived in peace with his memories in the city and never ran away from the responsibilities he left her with.

He changed the lives of everyone he met by living with someone as if they were good company, loving someone in their absence with no expectations, giving all rights to people who genuinely care, and providing relief to anyone who needed it.

His life was like a flower that endured everything, including the sun and thirst, before blooming and falling to the ground, spreading his fragrance.

www.ingramcontent.com/pod-product-compliance
Lightning Source LLC
Chambersburg PA
CBHW021144130726
47988CB00003B/1451